For Selah
—M.O.

For Lavanda
—L.L.

My Hair Is a Book
Text copyright © 2024 by Maisha Oso
Illustrations copyright © 2024 by London Ladd
All rights reserved. Manufactured in Italy.
No part of this book may be used or reproduced in any manner whatsoever without written permission except in the case of brief quotations embodied in critical articles and reviews. For information address HarperCollins Children's Books, a division of HarperCollins Publishers, 195 Broadway, New York, NY 10007.
www.harpercollinschildrens.com

Library of Congress Control Number: 2023948450
ISBN 978-0-06-324910-3

The artist used acrylic paint, cut paper, and tissue paper to create the illustrations for this book.
Typography by Chelsea C. Donaldson
24 25 26 27 28 RTLO 10 9 8 7 6 5 4 3 2 1

First Edition

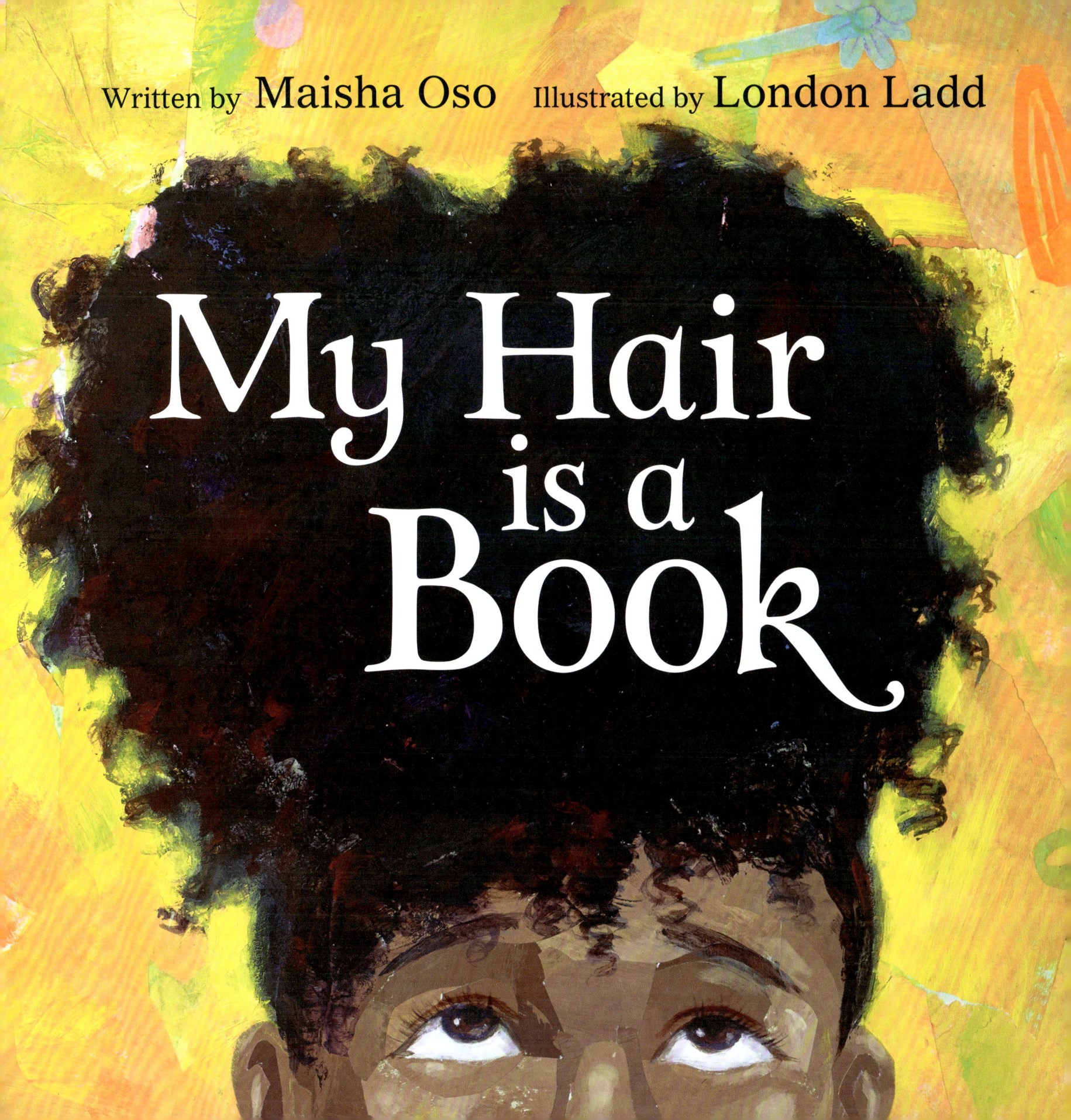

Written by **Maisha Oso** Illustrated by **London Ladd**

My Hair is a Book

My hair is a book.
Watch me open it,
part it,
take a look.

Thick,
   it's **packed** with centuries of history,
   millions of mysteries,

stories of people who look like me.

My hair tells **ponytails** of ancient tribes, Nubian vibes.

It **crowns** me the queen that I am.

My hair is a thesaurus.
There are so many words to describe it—
curly, **kinky**, and, of course, **coarse**.
No matter what you call it,
it's all good hair, Love.

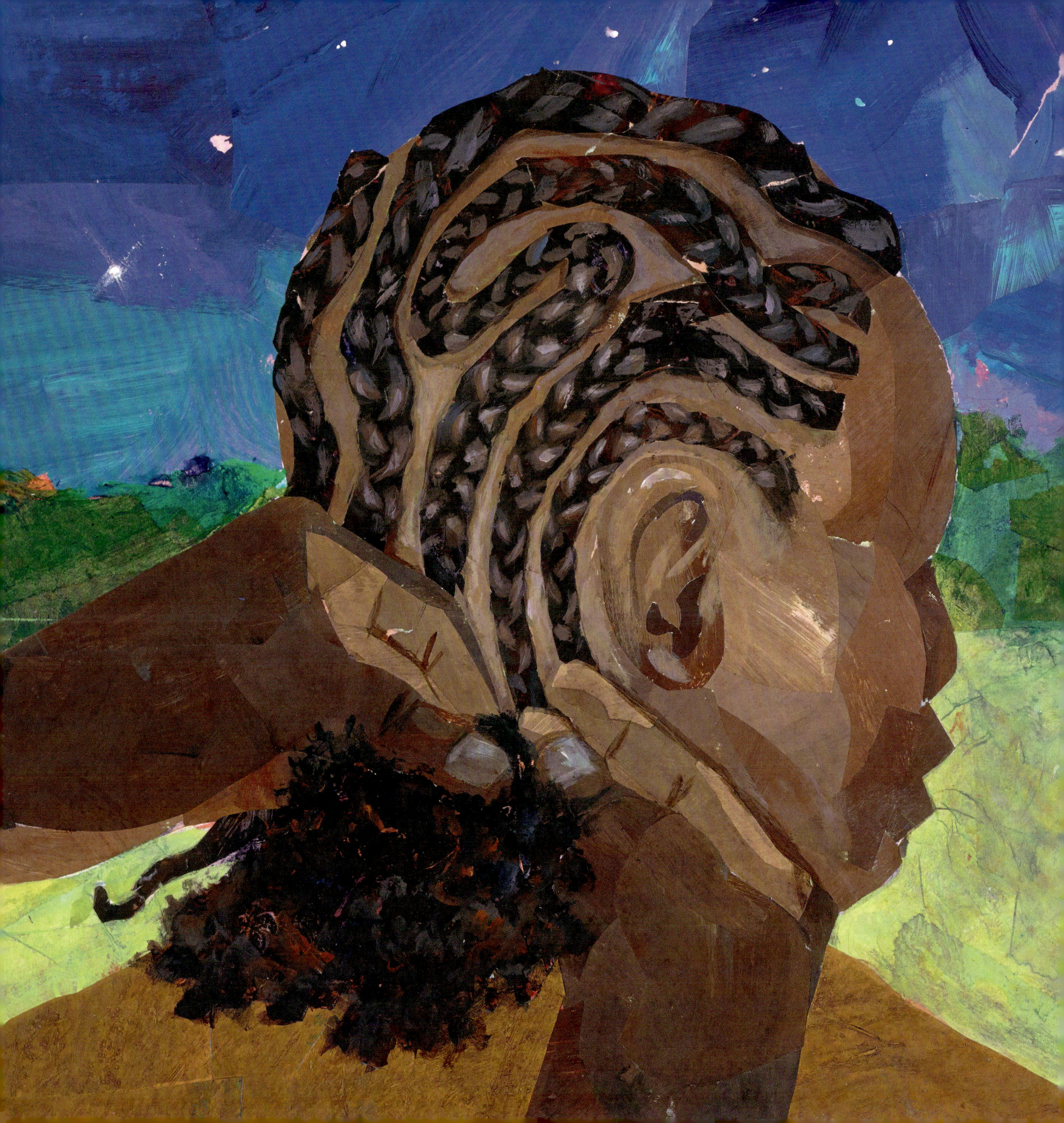

My hair is an atlas.

It contains maps to freedom.

Rows of corn guide me to escape the **locs** of chains.

Yeah, my *Roots* run that deep.

My hair is a book about dance—
It **twists** and **swoops**.

A book about sports—
it swings and hoops.
Curl it, **pin** it,
my hair loop de loops.

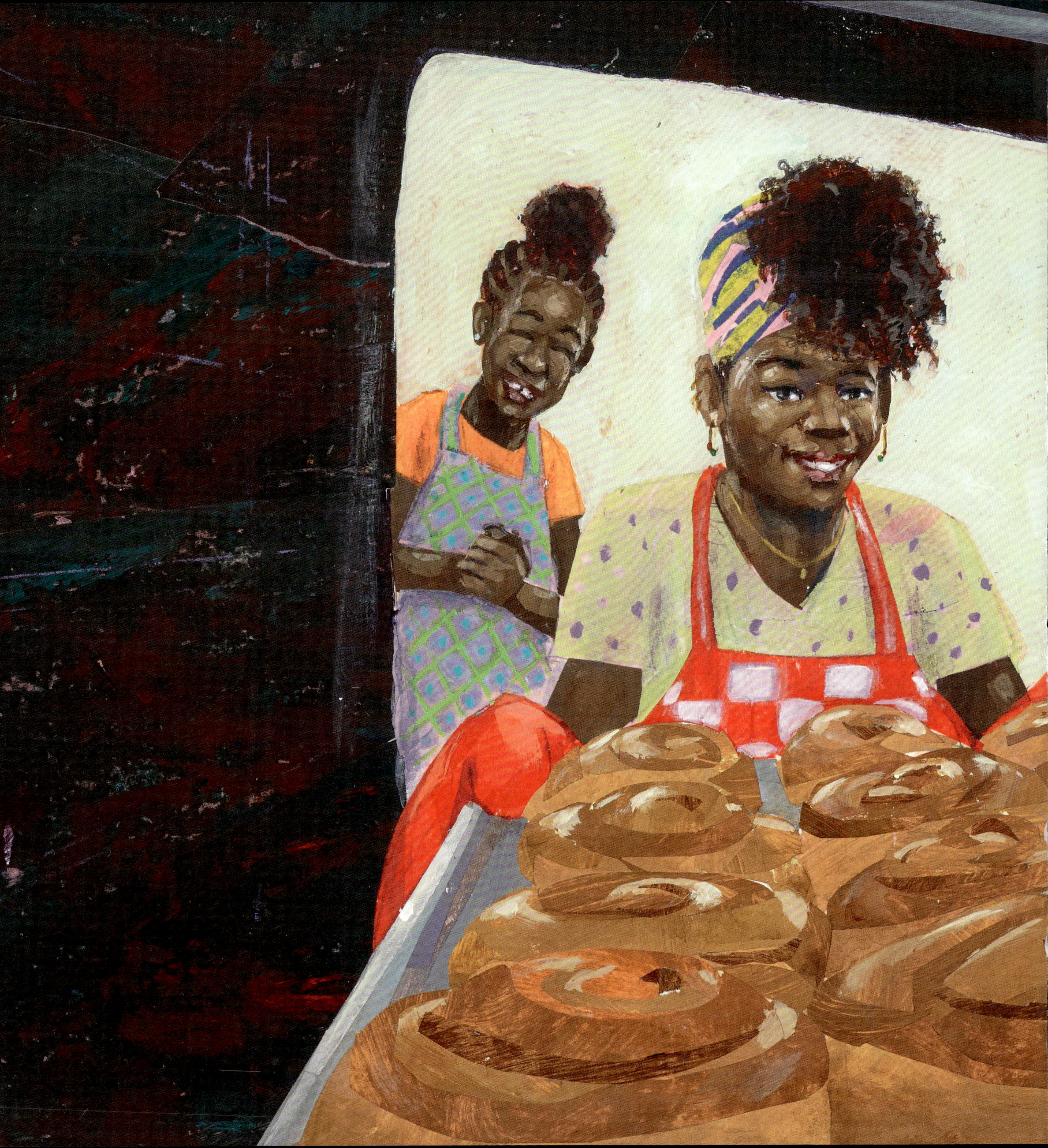

My hair is a cookbook
full of the sweetest recipes,
made for the hottest *kitchens*.

Cinna**buns** baked to a glistening brown,
a **pineapple updo** with curls falling down,
and you'll never get enough of my **Afro puffs**.
Everything you need
for a tasty **feed-in**.

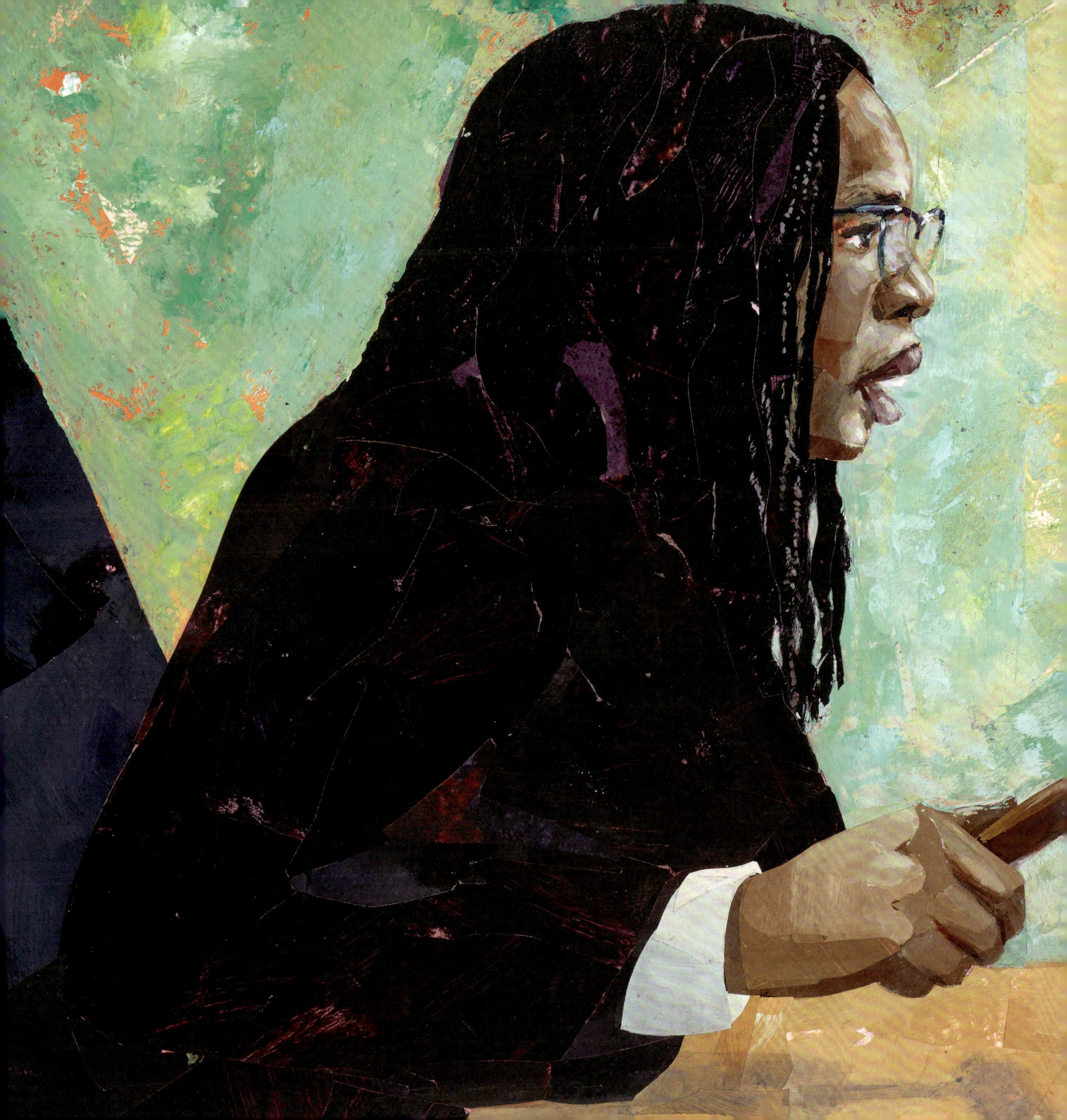

My hair is nonfiction like a textbook.
No matter the texture—**natural** or not,
short or long,
weak or strong,
my hair is the truth.
It's never wrong.

So if I decide to rock a **bob** or **Marley twists**,

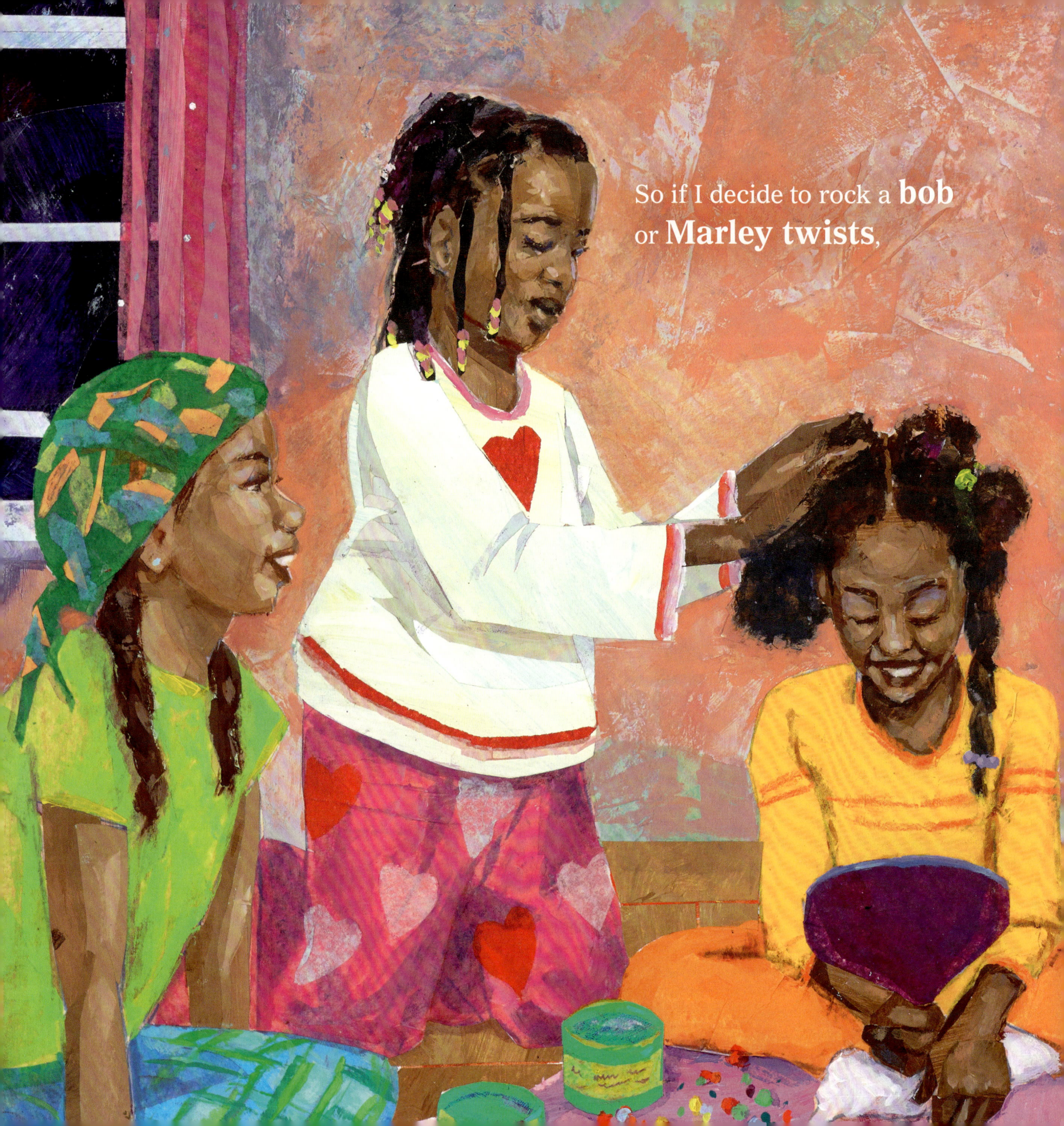

it's gonna be all right
'cause my hair is a whole mood.

My hair is a book that's stellar,
a bestseller,
hot off the **press**.
It reminds me that
I am every good thing.
I am more than enough.
My hair is undefeated!

Even with an appendix—
extensions, **wig**, or **weave**,
best believe
it's all mine.

So recognize perfection.
When your **finger waves** in my direction,
remember you can look but don't touch.

I love my hair so much.
And if they can't stand it,
picket, then ban it,
I'll still **pick** it, then **band** it,
'cause I understand that . . .

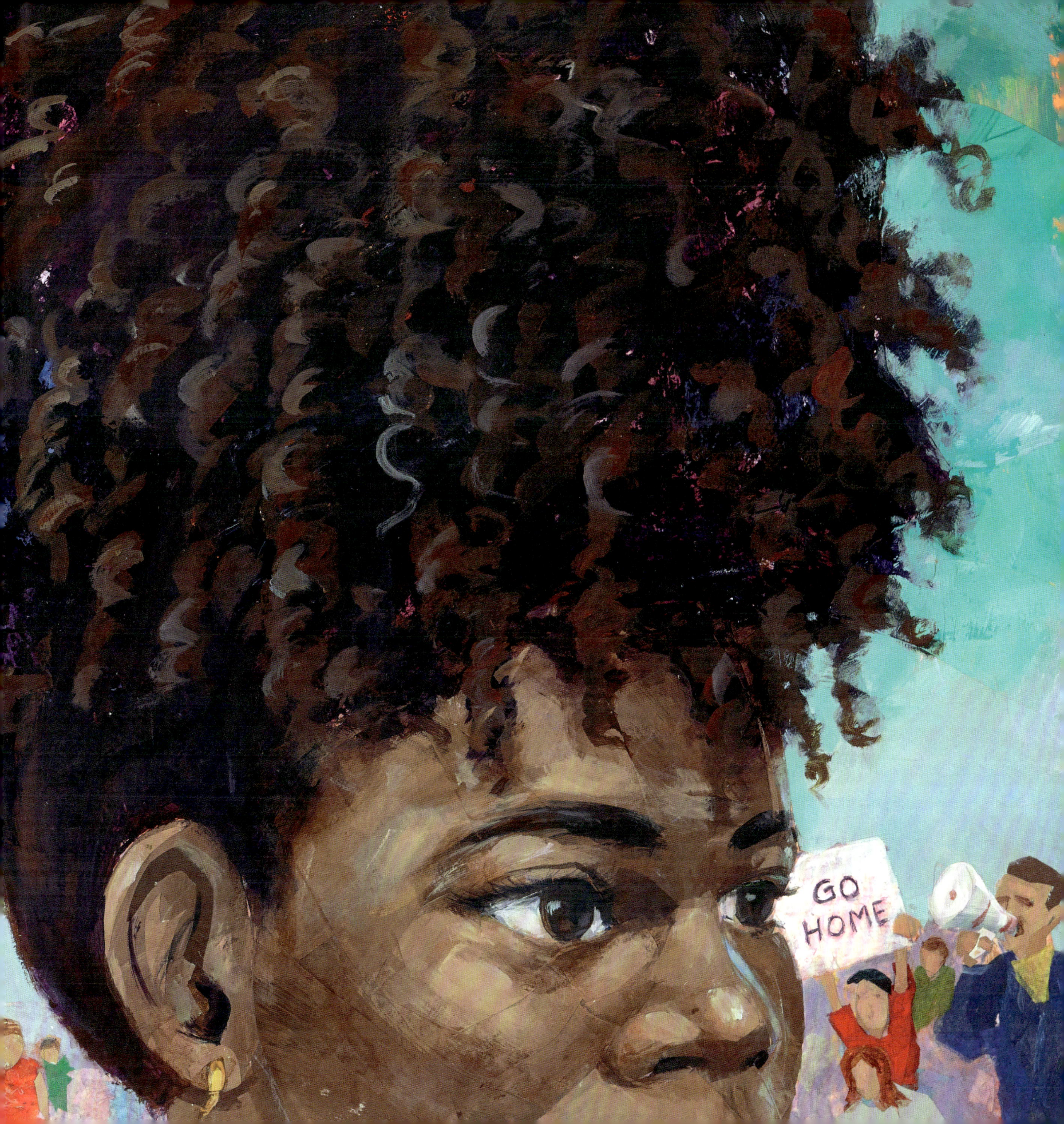
GO HOME

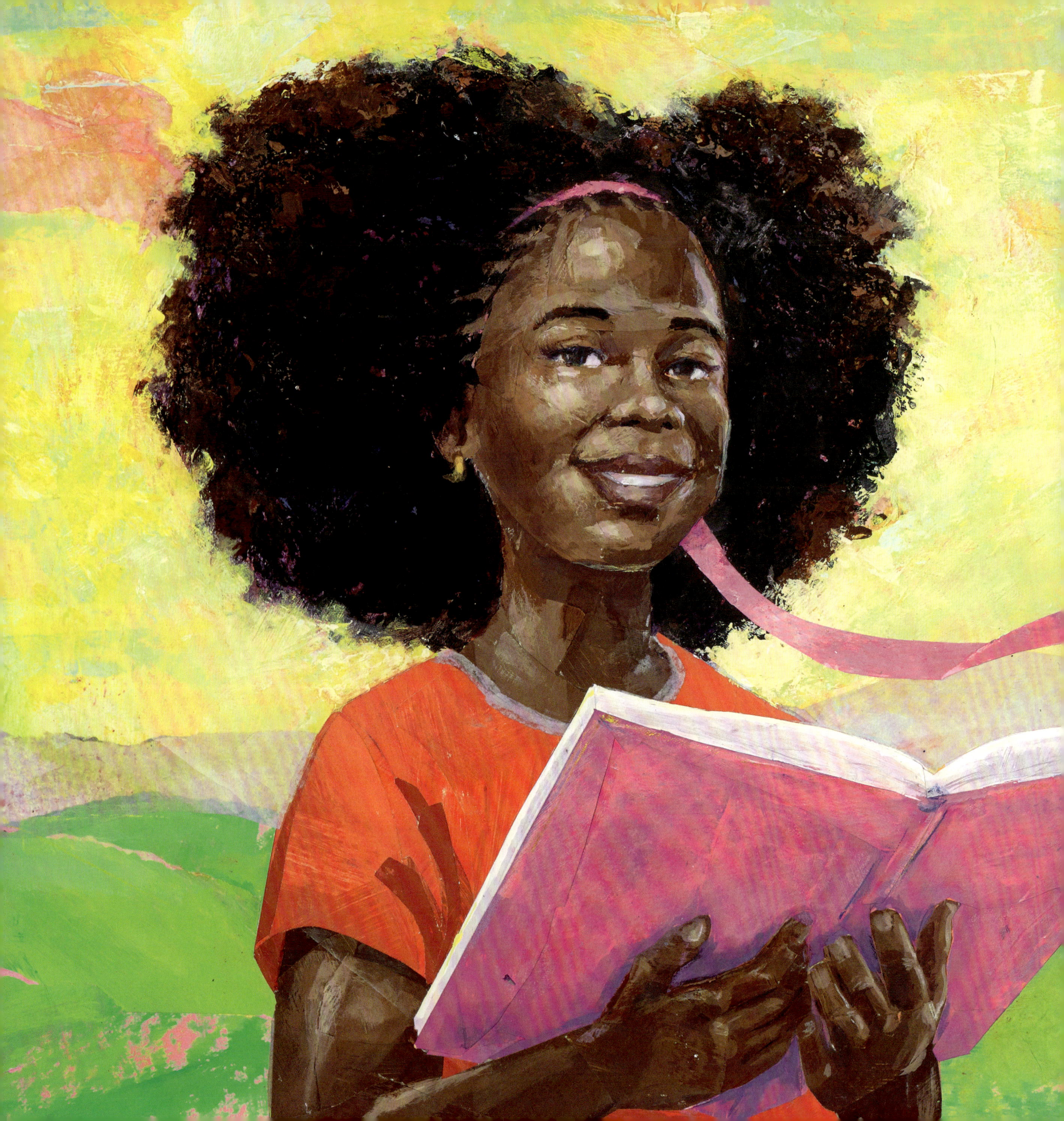

. . . my hair is a book,
and the title of that book is

Beautiful.

Author's Note

The first time I heard my daughter express any negative feelings about her hair, she was about three years old. It broke my heart. I had similar feelings about my own hair as a child—that it was too coarse, too thick, and not long enough. That's why I had been intentional about telling my daughter how wonderful her hair was. I explained to her countless times that its length, texture, every kink, and every curl were absolutely perfect. Still, with the television shows that she watched, the Disney princesses that she loved, and her friends at school, she was getting a message that hers wasn't as nice as everyone else's.

We are conditioned as a society to believe that "good" hair looks one specific way. So the unsaid implication is that if your hair is unlike the "good," it must be "bad." I wrote this book to reinforce the idea that all hair is "good" hair. It is my hope that a book that unapologetically celebrates Black hair in all of its curl patterns, textures, lengths, and styles will empower children like my daughter by helping them understand that their hair is beautiful exactly the way it is.

WITHDRAWN